Zookeeper for a Day

Puffin Books

Zookeeper for a Day

REBECCA JOHNSON

Illustrated by Kyla May

Puffin Books

PUFFIN BOOKS

Published by the Penguin Group
Penguin Group (Australia)
707 Collins Street, Melbourne, Victoria 3008, Australia
(a division of Penguin Australia Pty Ltd)
Penguin Group (USA) Inc.
375 Hudson Street, New York, New York 10014, USA
Penguin Group (Canada)
90 Eglinton Avenue East, Suite 700, Toronto, Canada ON M4P 2Y3
(a division of Penguin Canada Books Inc.)
Penguin Books Ltd
80 Strand, London WC2R 0RL England
Penguin Ireland
25 St Stephen's Green, Dublin 2, Ireland
(a division of Penguin Books Ltd)
Penguin Books India Pvt Ltd
11 Community Centre, Panchsheel Park, New Delhi – 110 017, India
Penguin Group (NZ)
67 Apollo Drive, Rosedale, Auckland 0632, New Zealand
(a division of Penguin New Zealand Pty Ltd)
Penguin Books (South Africa) (Pty) Ltd, Rosebank Office Park, Block D,
181 Jan Smuts Avenue, Parktown North, Johannesburg, 2196, South Africa
Penguin (Beijing) Ltd
7F, Tower B, Jiaming Center, 27 East Third Ring Road North,
Chaoyang District, Beijing 100020, China

Penguin Books Ltd, Registered Offices: 80 Strand, London, WC2R 0RL, England

First published by Penguin Group (Australia), 2014

1 3 5 7 9 10 8 6 4 2

Cover and text design by Karen Scott © Penguin Group (Australia)
Illustrations by Kyla May Productions
Typeset in New Century Schoolbook
Colour separation by Splitting Image Colour Studio, Clayton, Victoria
Printed and bound in Australia by Griffin Press, an accredited ISO AS/NZS 14001
Environmental Management Systems printer.

National Library of Australia Cataloguing-in-Publication data:

Johnson, Rebecca.
Zookeeper for a Day/Rebecca Johnson; illustrated by Kyla May.

ISBN: 978 0 14 330825 6 (pbk.)

A823.4

puffin.com.au

Hi! I'm Juliet. I'm ten years old.
And I'm nearly a vet!

I bet you're wondering how someone who is only ten could nearly be a vet. It's pretty simple really. My mum's a vet. I watch what she does and I help out all the time. There's really not that much to it, you know . . .

For my wonderful sister,
Narinda, who loves a good
adventure as much as I do.

X R

Dino Snaps

CHAPTER 1

Some vets work at zoos

I walk into the kitchen for breakfast and find my brother Max is hogging the whole table with little piles of cereal pieces.

'What *are* you doing, Max?' I ask.

'Playing with my food,' he says. 'It's a new cereal called Dino Snaps. Every piece is a little dinosaur packed full of fibre!'

I roll my eyes. He's obviously used the TV commercial to con Mum into buying them.

'Haven't you got enough dinosaurs without eating them as well?' I say, feeling a bit annoyed.

'She got you some too,' he says, fixing his line of iguanodons.

I sigh as I open the pantry. As if I care what shape my cereal is.

'Ooh, Zoo Snaps!' I say. They're shaped like cute little zoo animals! I turn the box around to look at the back and that's when I see it – *Want to be a zookeeper for a day?* It's a competition where you can win a day at the zoo with a real zookeeper.

I read the entry conditions out loud. 'In twenty-five words or less, tell us why you would make a great zookeeper.'

I whip my Vet Diary out of my back pocket. To be a vet, I have to have had experience with all kinds of animals. This is just what I need!

My best friend Chelsea, who lives next door, comes over just as I am jotting down some ideas.

'Chelsea, I'm going to win a competition where you get to be a zookeeper for a day, and you get to take a friend!' I show her the cereal box.

'That's *sooo* cool,' says Chelsea. 'You'd be perfect for that, Juliet. You're nearly a vet, so you'd be really helpful.'

'And imagine all the animals that would need grooming at a zoo, Chelsea.'

Chelsea frowns. 'I'm not sure about

brushing tigers . . .'

I laugh. 'I don't think they'll put us in with the tigers! Besides, if you're going to be a world-famous animal trainer and groomer one day, you'll have to get used to some tricky animals.'

'Imagine how great it would be?' says Chelsea.

'I know, we just have to win. We can enter as many times as we like, as long as each entry has a barcode from a box of Snaps cereal. Max and I both have one, so that's two entries already!'

We start working on our twenty-five-word entry forms right away.

'How does this sound?' I say after a while.

ZOOKEEPER FOR A DAY COMPETITION:

I am ten years old and nearly a vet. I know lots about farm animals and pets, but I really, really want to learn about zoo animals.

Sounds good to me,' says Chelsea. 'How many words is it?'

I count. 'Twenty-seven.'

We both look at the page. 'You could say *I'm* instead of *I am*. That would save one word. And maybe just say *ten* instead of *ten years old*. That will give us one word left we can use. How about *please*?'

'Perfect,' I say, and make the changes.

ZOOKEEPER FOR A DAY COMPETITION:

I'm ten and nearly a vet. I know lots about farm animals and pets, but I really, really want to learn about zoo animals. Please!

We fill in the two entry forms and walk them to the post box in the next street.

Now all we have to do is wait . . . and eat a whole lot more cereal.

CHAPTER 2

Vets can be disappointed

After weeks of eating *lots* of Zoo Snaps, finally it's the day of the competition draw.

Chelsea and I take the phone into the lounge room and watch animal movies so that we'll be right there when they call.

'Juliet speaking,' I say, when the phone rings at 2.00 p.m. Chelsea nods at me. She has her fingers crossed in her lap.

'Oh, hi Gran,' I say, trying not to

sound too disappointed. 'Mum's at the surgery and I'm waiting for a very important call. Can we call you back later?' I shake my head at Chelsea.

'Okay, Gran, love you too.'

We sit and wait all afternoon, but the phone doesn't ring again.

'I can't believe it,' says Chelsea, as she heads home for dinner. 'I thought we had a really good chance of winning.'

Even though it's Friday night, I go to bed early because I feel really grumpy and Max is annoying me.

The next morning I wake up to a terrible smell. Curly's rolled in chook poo again and he's standing beside my bed wagging his tail. I'm glad Chelsea's coming over. It looks like the first thing we will be doing is bathing Curly. Again.

The phone rings as we are up to our armpits in bubbles and dog hair. I'm holding Curly still in the laundry tub while Chelsea massages special apple-scented dog shampoo into his coat.

Max answers the phone. 'No, she can't come to the phone, she's busy.' He hangs up.

'Who was that Max?' says Mum.

'I don't know,' says Max, lining up his toy dinosaurs across the table. 'Someone wanting Juliet.'

Curly hears Mum's voice and tries

to leap out of the tub, just as the phone rings again. This time Mum gets it.

She comes into the laundry with a big smile on her face. 'Juliet, it's for you. It's Susan calling from Snaps Cereal.'

I'm so excited that I let go of Curly and he leaps out of the laundry tub and runs through the house shaking and barking. I can hardly hear the

lady on the phone. She tells me that I HAVE WON!

'We won! They say we can go next Saturday,' I say to Chelsea and Mum as soon as I get off the phone. 'We're going to be zookeepers!' Chelsea and I jump around the laundry. Mum is really excited for us too.

'We're going to be so busy getting our zoo kits ready in time!' I say.

CHAPTER 3

Vets need to make a good impression

'Have you remembered all your different combs?' I say to Chelsea the night before we go. 'There will be heaps of different hair types.'

'Uh-huh,' says Chelsea. 'And I've got a notebook for writing down training tips.'

'Good thinking,' I say.

We go to bed early because we have to be at the zoo at 7 a.m. and it's a long drive. Mum's going to take us, so Chelsea gets to sleep over.

Mum looks at my bulging vet kit as I walk out to the car the next morning.

'You know, Juliet, you won't need that today. The zoo vets will have everything they need.'

'Mum,' I say. 'How many times has my vet kit come in handy? I'm not taking any chances. The reason we won is because they know I'm nearly a vet, so the least they will expect is for me to have my own kit. We're going to impress them with how helpful we can be.'

'Oh, I'm sure you'll make an impression all right,' says Dad as he puts Chelsea's grooming kit into the car.

When we get to the zoo, Mum comes

in with us to sign forms and check when she should pick us up. We're going to be here until 3 p.m! That's seven hours of zoo time!

We start by showing Peter, our zookeeper for the day, our vet kits. He's so impressed he doesn't know what to say. He just looks at Mum with big eyes.

'It's going to be really crazy here today,' he says to Mum. 'Sabula, one of our elephants, is due to have her first calf. The vets have been with her all night and it looks like it's going to happen today.'

'Those vets will have their hands full,' Mum says.

'It's lucky Juliet is here,' says Chelsea.

The keeper looks a bit confused.

'She's nearly a vet,' Chelsea explains.

We kiss Mum goodbye and turn back to Peter. He gives us both a 'Zookeeper for a Day' T-shirt and we race off to put them on.

'Right,' I say when we get back. 'Where do we start?'

Peter tells us that the first thing we will be doing is checking the animals are all safe and well after the night. As he speaks I make a list in my Vet Diary.

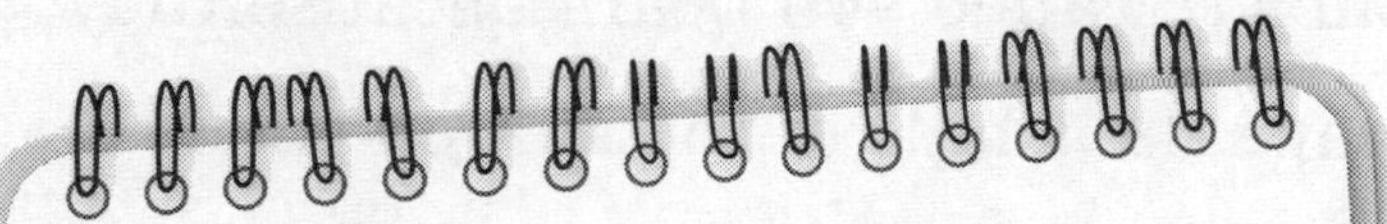

ZOOKEEPER JOBS:

- Check on animals after night-time in their inside enclosures.
- Make sure they have no injuries.

Our first stop is the sun bears.

'I didn't realise how much of a zoo you don't see when you visit,' says Chelsea as we walk down the corridors behind all the cages.

The bears are very happy to see Peter. He taps his hand on the wire mesh and one of them stands up and puts her paws against the wire. Her long hooked nails poke through the wire and Chelsea takes a step back.

'Did you know, Chelsea, that they're called sun bears because they have the shape of the sun on their necks?' I say.

Peter nods and gives me a smile. He opens a container on his hip and scoops out some white gooey stuff with his fingers.

'Ew, what's that?' yelps Chelsea. 'I don't think I can watch!'

Peter stares at her for a moment. 'It's porridge.'

'Oh,' smiles Chelsea, biting her lip.

Peter puts his fingers up against the wire and the sun bear licks the porridge from them.

'Lots of zoo animals are trained to stand up like this, so we can check their undersides for injuries. It's called *target training*,' he explains, 'and it gets the animals used to having the vets treat them without being sedated.'

Chelsea has her notebook out and

is writing furiously. 'I could try that on Princess, my cat,' she says.

I bob down to get a closer look at the bears' tummies as each one stands up. 'They all look fine, Peter,' I say.

Suddenly the door opens and a vet in surgical clothes comes rushing into the room. His name tag says 'Ben'.

'Peter, we need a hand with the giraffes. Kamu has torn his ear overnight and we need the others out of the way. I'm short on time because Sabula could have the calf at any time.'

'Right,' says Peter, and we're off.

CHAPTER 4

Vets should always be prepared

Chelsea and I struggle to keep up as Peter and Ben stride along the path towards the giraffe enclosure.

'Wow, I thought the bears were big!' gasps Chelsea when we get there. 'They are so beautiful up close.'

The giraffes are bunched in a corner. Their long, graceful necks cross over each other as they look at us. The largest one has a small patch of blood on his ear. It's hard to see from all the way down here.

'I don't know what he's cut it on or how bad it is, but I need to take a look,' says Ben. 'Can you get the others down the end and we'll try to get Kamu into the crush?'

'Sure,' says Peter, and we trot off after him.

'Why would they want to crush him?' whispers Chelsea.

'A crush is a special narrow pen where they can stop the animal from moving around, Chelsea,' Peter says, laughing. She looks very relieved.

Peter grabs some carrots and climbs up to a tall platform. 'You can come up with me,' he calls down, 'but one at a time.'

'You go up, Chelsea,' I say. 'I want to watch the vet.'

I walk back to where some other keepers are helping to separate Kamu from the giraffes and herd him into a small pen. I can't help but peek into Ben's vet kit lying open on the ground. It's very impressive and has instruments I haven't seen in Mum's surgery. I might need to get myself some new supplies.

I hear Chelsea giggling and look over to see her on the high platform with Peter, feeding carrots to the giraffes. Their long blue tongues wrap around the carrots and pull them into their mouths. 'Ew yuk!' she squeaks, as giraffe slobber drips on her shorts. She won't be happy about that.

Ben has climbed to the platform beside the crush and is now looking at Kamu's ear. Another keeper is feeding carrots to the patient and a vet nurse stands by to pass equipment up to Ben.

'Ah, I see what the problem is,' says Ben to the nurse below. 'He's got a huge splinter. He must have been rubbing his head against the trees or something. Can you pass me my tweezers, please?'

The vet nurse looks around in the kit. 'Can you remember where you put them? They're not in the usual spot.'

'Oh, blast. I left them in the steriliser after I stitched that water buffalo. Can you run and get them?'

'I have tweezers!' I say, throwing my vet kit open. 'And I sterilised them in my mum's surgery just before we came.'

They all look over, as if noticing me for the first time.

'I'm Juliet,' I say, shrugging. 'I'm nearly a vet.'

'Well, Juliet, *nearly* a vet,' says the vet nurse, smiling, 'you'd better take your sterile tweezers up to Ben, *really* a vet.'

I cannot believe my luck! I told mum my vet kit would come in handy. I just knew it. I can't get the smile off my face as I climb the ladder and pass the vet my tweezers.

I'm about to climb down when Ben says, 'You can't leave now. This could end up being a two-vet job, you know!'

I look over at Chelsea brushing a giraffe's neck and give her a tiny wave and a huge smile. Right now, all our dreams have just come true.

Ben carefully pulls out the large splinter (I'm allowed to keep it!) and I dab some antiseptic cream on Kamu's ear before we climb down the ladder.

I proudly return my tweezers to my kit and put the splinter in a specimen jar, then I snap the kit shut.

'Well, it's a lucky thing we have another vet on duty today,' smiles Ben. 'We might need a hand if this baby elephant decides to finally make an entrance today.' He ruffles my hair, picks up his kit and heads off.

'I can't wait to be a real vet,' I whisper under my breath.

'Okay,' says Peter, appearing beside me. 'We'd better clean out these enclosures before we let the animals out of their night stalls. The zoo will open soon and the visitors aren't going to like it if all they can see are piles of dung.'

I whip out my diary and turn to the page of zookeeper jobs.

ZOOKEEPER JOBS:

- Check on animals after night-time in their inside enclosures.
- Make sure they have no injuries.
- Pick up dung.

Peter hands us each a scoop and a bucket as we enter the red panda enclosure. The panda looks at us through the bars of its night cage as we walk around scooping up droppings. Peter follows us, raking the sand.

'Chelsea, if you keep holding your breath, you're going to faint!' I laugh.

She says nothing, but she shakes her head quickly. It's hard to speak when your cheeks are full of air.

'I know,' says Peter to the gorgeous panda as it looks out at us. 'We're a bit late with breakfast this morning, but the girls are going to get it for you as soon as we're finished.'

I grab a specimen jar out of my vet

kit and use a stick to poke some red panda poo into it.

I look up to see Peter staring at me with an odd look on his face.

'I have a scat collection,' I explain. 'I have droppings from twenty-three different animals already at home. You know, you can learn an awful lot about an animal from its poo.'

'Well, I've never met one like you before,' says Peter, shaking his head.

I smile. I think he likes me.

CHAPTER 5

Zoo animals eat a lot!

We head into the zoo kitchen and it is super busy. The amount of food that is being cut up is incredible.

Peter can see we're amazed. There are huge tubs of fruit, vegetables, pellets and grain spread out around us, and each staff member is carefully reading clipboards and weighing amounts of food before putting them into labelled trays.

'Will they eat all of this in one week?' I ask.

'Oh, no,' laughs Peter. 'This is just for one day! There's also a meat locker for all the carnivores and an insect room where the maggots, mealworms, crickets and other insects are raised.'

I whip out my Vet Diary as Peter keeps talking.

ZOO KITCHEN FACTS:

- More kinds of food are served in a zoo than in most restaurants.
- Zoos buy huge amounts of grain, fruit, vegetables, meat, fish, and other foods. In one year this zoo uses 19,000 eggs and 54,000 carrots.
- Some animals are picky eaters in nature and need special diets. A famous example is the koala, which eats only the fresh leaves of eucalyptus trees.
- Many animals eat their food as it comes, but some need their food measured, chopped, combined, or even cooked.

'I'm going to leave you girls here to help prepare some meals for the animals while I go and finish raking and cleaning enclosures,' says Peter.

'Oh, hang on, Peter,' I say, reaching for some specimen jars from my vet kit. 'Can you get me some more scat samples, please?'

Peter looks at me for a minute, then smiles and takes the jars. I bet he's going to want to start his own scat collection now I've given him the idea.

'Please don't make me touch a maggot, Juliet,' whispers Chelsea in my ear.

Chelsea and I help the zoo staff with preparing the food for the red panda, penguins, sun bears, tamarins, otters, iguanas and the bamboo partridges. I make a page for each in my diary for when we go to visit them so I can write down any facts.

Whilst Chelsea cuts the fruit and vegetables into very neat little pieces, I go with a lady called Stacey to the room where all the insects are being bred.

The smell is disgusting! I pull a face and slap my hand over my mouth. It's lucky that Chelsea didn't come too.

'Gotta get used to bad smells if you want to work with animals,' says Stacey gruffly. We scoop some mealworms (which are not actually worms at all, but beetle larvae) into little dishes and collect some fly pupae (these are maggots in cocoons turning into flies!). We also grab a couple of containers of crickets.

'Not many animals actually like maggots,' says Stacey as I peer into the tank full of writhing white fly larvae, 'but lots of them love the pupae.'

I couldn't imagine eating anything worse.

As we come out of the insect room, a man returns with a large tub of porridge.

'Did she eat anything?' asks Stacey.

'No,' says the big man. 'Ben hopes she's not far off now, so fingers crossed. She's having a lot of trouble.'

Chelsea and I know they are talking about the baby elephant being born. 'Imagine if we got to see a newborn elephant calf!' I say.

Stacey overhears me. 'They won't let you anywhere near that calf today. The public won't see it till the end of the week.' She walks back into the insect room.

'We're not the public!' says Chelsea. 'Juliet, you're nearly a vet. You've already helped out once today.'

Peter comes back in and we load up our cart to go and feed some animals.

I really hope we do get to see the baby elephant if it's born soon.

Our first stop is the tamarin

monkeys. They are so cute and little. Peter lets us come in with him and we sit quietly on the ground. The little monkeys know Peter and climb straight up onto his shoulders. He passes them mealworms and they gobble them down like chocolates. Chelsea screws up her nose, but smiles.

A young tamarin creeps over and sits at our feet.

'Hold your hands out flat and put some peas on them,' says Peter quietly. I slowly put my hand into the dish and hold it out with a small pile of peas. The little monkey holds my thumb with his tiny hand and pops the peas into his mouth, watching us the whole time.

'He's so cute,' whispers Chelsea.

'We'd better keep moving,' says Peter. 'There are lots of hungry mouths to feed!' He fills their bowls with clean water and fresh food.

'Can you grab a box of crickets from the cart, Juliet,' he says. 'We'll let them go in here to give these little guys something to hunt. It's really important to keep zoo animals busy so they don't get bored.'

I grab the crickets and pull the lid off just as a monkey leaps past and knocks the box from my hand. Crickets leap in every direction, including into Chelsea's hair!

The monkeys go crazy chasing the crickets around. Chelsea goes crazy too.

'Juliet! Juliet! They're in my hair!' she gasps, frantically trying to sweep the crickets off as they scurry for a hiding spot. 'Get them off! Get them off!'

Peter and I do our best to get them all off her, but she is still a little shaken

when we leave the pen. Her hair is the messiest I've ever seen it.

'Oh dear,' whimpers Chelsea. 'I don't like crickets. I really don't like crickets. Can you see any more in my hair?'

'It's okay now, Chelsea,' I soothe, trying my best to fix her hair. Chelsea always has really, really neat hair.

'They're all gone and your hair looks fine, doesn't it, Peter?'

'Sure,' says Peter, nodding his head and trying not to smile.

Next we visit the red panda again. Peter fills her bowls and we help tie flowers and bamboo to the trees. I scribble a few quick notes:

RED PANDA FOOD:
- berries
- flowers
- bamboo
- eggs

Then we're off to the bamboo partridge enclosure. We sprinkle seeds, nuts, grapes, diced fruit and a few mealworms on the ground. The pretty brown and tan birds scurry around to eat them. Peter hangs some orange halves in the trees for them to find.

The animals' food looks so fresh and lovely that my tummy starts to rumble. It must be nearly time for morning tea. Zookeepers work really hard.

CHAPTER 6

Vets need to eat too

We push our cart around the path behind Peter, stopping every now and then to feed the animals on our list. There are so many creatures at the zoo and each keeper is responsible for cleaning and feeding different ones. Peter has to feed even more today because extra people are helping with the baby elephant birth.

Next we throw lettuce into the iguana enclosure. Max would love these guys, because the huge lizards really do look like living dinosaurs.

'Otters and penguins are next,' says Peter, 'and then we'll stop for some morning tea.'

To feed the otters, Peter has to put on long rubber pants called waders and a big coat and gloves. It's really slippery in there and Peter tells us that otters might look very cute, but they have sharp teeth and can give a nasty bite. He takes a bucket of crayfish in and hides them amongst the rocks. The otters scurry around poking their little black faces with long whiskers into all the rock crevices.

'That should keep them busy for a

while,' he says as he comes back out.

The Australian little penguins are next door, and this time we're allowed to come in. Peter shows us how to hold the tiny dead fish by the tail so that they go down the penguins' throats headfirst. They love them and crowd around us like little men in fancy suits.

'I can't believe we're doing this!' I say to Chelsea. 'It was *soooo* worth eating all that cereal!'

'Hey, Mum, look at that!'

A boy with an ice-cream is looking over the fence at us. Chelsea and I laugh and wave. It feels very cool being on the other side of the fence.

‘Hey, what’s wrong with my fish?’ Chelsea asks. The penguins look at it as she dangles it over their beaks, then they turn away.

‘It’s because it’s bent,’ laughs Peter. ‘These penguins are very picky with the fish they eat. They won't eat any fish that are bent or damaged.'

'I think they might be a bit spoilt,' sniffs Chelsea, and I think she might be right. She does know a lot about training animals.

We wash the fish from our fingers and I make a quick couple of notes.

PENGUIN FOOD FACTS:

- Penguins like to eat their fish headfirst so the fins don't get stuck in their throats.
- They don't like their fish to be bent or damaged.

For morning tea, Peter takes us to the animal enrichment area. This is where they make things to keep the animals entertained.

'A bored animal is an unhealthy animal,' I explain to Chelsea.

We make some toys for the animals as we eat our snacks. Peter goes off to check on the elephant.

The first thing we make is for the capuchin monkeys. Leisa, another zookeeper, shows us how to put walnuts into the bottom of plastic containers and cover the tops with masking tape.

'The monkeys will use the rocks in their enclosures to break through the tape,' she explains, 'and then they eat the nuts.'

'Animals are so clever,' says Chelsea. I agree.

We start on the toys for the bears. They love to rummage and hunt for their food, so we help Leisa hide food in their toys. It's great fun. Mine look a bit messy when we're finished, but Chelsea's are all very colourful and neat. I wonder if the bears will notice the difference.

I make a list in my diary of the things we've made, so I can tell Mum later.

THINGS TO KEEP BEARS FROM GETTING BORED:

- Plastic bottles with grapes and raisins in them.
- Hard plastic plumbing pipes with coconuts full of porridge inside.
- Hollow bamboo stalks stuffed with dry biscuits.
- Pine cones smeared with sticky treats like peanut butter or honey.
- Hollow plastic toys filled with treats and frozen into popsicles.
- Hard plastic balls smeared with peanut butter or jam for them to lick off.

When Peter comes back from the elephant area, he looks worried.

'She's really struggling,' he says to Leisa. 'I think they're getting pretty concerned.' The zookeepers talk for a while in low voices and I try to listen.

'Oh no, Juliet!' Chelsea startles me when she whispers in my ear. She sounds quite upset.

'I'm sure the elephant and her calf will be fine,' I tell her.

'It's not that. I think I have a cricket in my shirt still. It's driving me crazy. I can feel it. Will you have a look?'

We duck off to the toilet and I look in Chelsea's shirt. 'I'm sure you're just imagining it,' I say when I see nothing there. 'Remember when Bertie Brownstone had head lice and you washed your hair six times in one night? It'll be just like that. There are no crickets on you, I promise.'

When we come out, Peter is waiting for us.

'Boy, have I got a job for you two,' he says.

I run to grab my kit. 'Come on, Chelsea!' I say. 'It might be time to brush that tiger!'

CHAPTER 7

Vets need a lot of help

'It's time to scrub a tortoise,' says Peter.

'Now that sounds like fun,' says Chelsea, grabbing her grooming kit.

Peter takes us to the grassy area where the huge Galápagos tortoises roam around nibbling the grass.

'This is Grandpa,' he says. 'He's 142 years old!'

Chelsea and I fall in love with Grandpa immediately. He's huge! Peter tells us some facts about him and I write them down.

GRANDPA THE GALAPAGOS TORTOISE:

- Grandpa weighs just under 400kg.
- He is 1.5m long!
- He has been at the zoo since it opened and originally came from the London Zoo.
- Grandpa's very friendly.

'Now,' says Peter, 'Grandpa here is getting a bit too old to go for swims in the pond these days, and we like to keep his shell nice and clean for him. Do you think you could give him a bit of a scrub?'

'Are you kidding?' I laugh. 'Chelsea is nearly a world-famous animal trainer and groomer. We'll have

Grandpa looking shiny in no time.'

'I thought you might,' Peter smiles. 'Here's a bucket of lettuce and fruit for Grandpa. If you put this in front of him he'll stay nice and still for you. I've got to go and do some more cleaning jobs, but Marcia is just over there,' he points to a lady trimming a hedge, 'and she can radio if you need me.'

'Thanks, Peter,' we say together.

'I bet he's going to check on the elephant,' I say as he walks off. 'I think there's a problem. Vets have a special sense for these things.'

'They'll look after her,' says Chelsea. 'Come on, let's get busy!' She snaps open her kit on the grass.

We scrub and rub and clean and scrape. We use toothbrushes to get into all the tight places and steel wool to buff up the dry, flaky spots. Chelsea even gives Grandpa a manicure. He loves it and just keeps on munching. Every now and then he stretches his neck up really tall and looks around.

'He's doing that because he wants his neck washed as well,' says Chelsea. We do a great job on that too.

Chelsea takes some rags out of her kit and finally we polish his shell.

When Peter comes back he is amazed. 'Wow,' he says. 'Grandpa has never looked so clean. He looks eighty years younger!'

Marcia comes over to have a look too. They are both very impressed, especially with the lovely blue ribbon we Blu Tacked to his shell.

'Ready to go and feed some babies?' Peter asks us.

Could this day get any better? We gather our kits and head to the animal nursery. It's not even lunchtime yet and we're both exhausted, but there's no way we want to stop for a rest.

When Peter takes us into the nursery we have to be really quiet. There are a few cages with some sick animals in them, but I am pleased that most of them are empty. One of the cages has a large, colourful bird in it. It doesn't look well. The vet nurse is giving it some medicine from a dropper.

'That's a macaw,' says Peter. 'He's a bit sick at the moment, but Sophie will get him back on the mend.' Sophie looks over and gives us a smile and motions that we can come closer.

'I'm Juliet,' I whisper.

'She's nearly a vet,' says Peter. 'And this is Chelsea. She's nearly an animal trainer and groomer.'

'Well, how lucky that you're here,' says Sophie. 'We're short-staffed today and I could use some help from people with experience.'

‘What can we help with?’ I say, as I pop open my kit.

‘Well,’ says Sophie, clearly impressed, ‘as soon as I’ve finished this job I need to bathe a very dirty little Tasmanian devil and then entertain some cheeky baby meerkats. Do either of those jobs interest you?’

Our eyes must nearly pop out of our heads because Peter and Sophie burst out laughing.

CHAPTER 8

Vets have some lovely jobs

Sophie carefully uncovers a tiny little Tasmanian devil that is in a carry crate. It is about the size of a six-week-old puppy and is so cute. He is covered in mud and has some fur missing from his back.

Sophie gently lifts him out of the crate in a towel. He opens his mouth as if to hiss, but no sound comes out. He thinks he's so fierce.

'Now let's have a look at you, Buster,' she says. 'One of the keepers noticed this little joey was extra muddy and had some fur missing. We just want to clean him up and check him for cuts before we give him back to his mum.'

Sophie gets Chelsea and me to prepare a basin of warm water, and she holds Buster while we gently sponge the dirt off his fur. The little devil looks up at us with his small black eyes.

'I'll do the area where the hair is missing,' says Sophie.

She has a closer look at him. 'No cuts. Probably just play fighting with your brothers and sisters,' she says to the little devil. 'Tasmanian devils are pretty tough on each other. It's a battle to survive from the minute they're born.'

We dry him off with a warm towel and wrap him up like a baby. Buster goes to sleep in Chelsea's arms.

Sophie calls another zookeeper to tell her that Buster's fine to go back to his mum, and we put him back into his crate.

'Now,' she says, 'are you ready to meet my ratbags?'

She takes us into another room where there is a playpen on the ground. 'Shhh,' she says as she steps in and motions for us to follow. We sit down on the blanket beside her.

Sophie taps her fingers on the top of a plastic box with a hole in it, and we hear movement inside.

'Watch this,' she says.

All of a sudden three little heads fill the doorway and peep out at us.

'Baby meerkats!' I can hardly control my excitement.

'Come on,' whispers Sophie to the shy babies. 'Come on.' She rolls a tennis ball on the blanket and they all watch it closely.

They are little balls of fluff with grey heads, honey-coloured bodies and long skinny tails. They bounce out across the floor towards the ball and jump all over it, tumbling over the top of each other. Every now and then, one of them tries to stand up on its back legs, then gets bowled over by another. They *really are* the cutest things I have ever seen.

The babies start racing around and climbing onto our legs then leaping off.

'Why are they here?' I ask, as Sophie gently scoops one up and hands it to me.

'Their mum rejected them for some reason. We don't know why, but sometimes that happens in nature.' The little meerkat starts to lick my thumb.

'They're due for a feed,' says Sophie. 'Can you girls play with them while I warm up their bottles? These babies are going to be part of our zoo education program, so they need to get used to people.'

‘Will they ever go back in with the other meerkats?’

‘I’m afraid not,’ says Sophie. ‘Meerkats are very territorial and would chase them away and possibly hurt them.’

Sophie returns a minute later with three warm little bottles.

‘We’ve done something like this before,’ I say. ‘After a bushfire, we had to help my mum. She’s a vet. We had to feed a whole lot of orphaned sugar gliders and possums.’

‘I knew you girls would be a great help!’ Sophie says.

We sit together on the floor and give the baby meerkats their bottles.

Chelsea strokes hers with her finger and we look at each other and smile.

Every so often, Chelsea scratches herself and looks uncomfortable.

'I still think I've got crickets on me,' she whispers.

'No, you haven't,' I say.

Peter comes in and tells us we will be having a special guest join us for lunch.

We thank Sophie, kiss our meerkats goodbye, grab our kits and head off. I knew zoos were busy places, but this is ridiculous!

We walk into a large room with a table set up in front of a large cage. There are some sandwiches on plates for us, but I can only see stools for three people.

'I thought we were having a guest?' says Chelsea.

'You are,' says Peter. 'I'm just getting his lunch.' He walks out of the room and comes back with a very big piece of meat hooked onto a chain. He opens a door in the cage and hangs the meat up on the mesh. Then he locks the cage and speaks to someone on his radio.

CHAPTER 9

Vets get scared too

'Let him in, Tom, we're good to go.'

Chelsea nearly falls off her seat when a huge Sumatran tiger pads into the cage in front of us from a side door. I must admit, for a moment I panic too.

'This is Rabu,' says Peter, 'and he's going to have lunch with us.'

The three of us sit and eat sandwiches while we watch the massive tiger eat his enormous piece of meat. It is the scariest thing I've ever seen, but it's exciting too.

When Rabu's finished, he licks himself, yawns and stretches, then heads back out the door he came in.

'He's going outside for a sleep in the sun,' says Peter.

'They really are just big cats, aren't they?' says Chelsea. 'Princess does that after she eats too.'

‘What do we do now?’ I say, feeling a little sleepy myself.

‘We need to take a load of hay to the zebras and deer,’ says Peter. ‘Then it will be just about time for your mum to come and get you.’

‘In case I forget to tell you later, Peter, we’ve had the BEST day,’ I say.

Chelsea nods in agreement.

As we are loading the hay, I can’t help notice that Peter keeps looking towards the elephant house. I can see he’s worried, but he doesn’t say anything. Vets and zookeepers must get really attached to the animals they care for.

We’re allowed to ride on the buggy

with him as it tows the load of hay towards the plains animals' area.

Peter's radio crackles and we hear a man's voice over the motor of the buggy.

'Change of plan,' says Peter, smiling, and he turns the vehicle around.

'Has the baby been born?' I ask.

'Is it okay?' says Chelsea.

'Whoa, slow down!' laughs Peter. 'Let's just go and have a look, hey?'

We stop outside a huge barn and tiptoe inside behind Peter. There are lots of zookeepers there, but they are all watching very quietly. We all stand behind the rails of a massive fence and peer through.

I let out a gasp.

There, on the ground, is a tiny baby elephant. It looks so little compared to its mother. The only movement is its little sausage-like trunk flicking gently up and down.

'The calf is very weak because the mother has had so much trouble having her,' whispers Peter. 'The vets are waiting to see if she'll need help standing up to feed. Her mother will try to help her.'

I hold onto Chelsea's arm. Already you can see how much the mother elephant loves her baby. She runs her enormous trunk over her calf's little body, as if she's checking it's all right.

'Please get up, little one,' whispers a young zookeeper beside me. It feels as if all of us are holding our breath.

The little calf struggles and falls so many times. She just can't seem to do it. The mother elephant tries to help her with her trunk, but the baby keeps slipping and falling. She doesn't have the strength to stand.

She's so beautiful. Her little ears and body are a perfect mini version of her mother. She looks so gorgeous. If only she could stand.

The other elephants are all looking through the bars at her, and like us they are silent and worried.

'Time to step in, I think,' says Ben,

the vet I helped with the giraffes. He and three other men slowly climb into the yard. The mother elephant looks at them warily and swings her trunk from side to side. She keeps looking down at her baby.

Peter passes them a large piece of fabric.

'Good girl, Sabula,' says Ben, as he walks over to the mother and strokes her cheek. 'Let us help you get this baby to her feet.'

The four men gently pass the fabric under the calf's tummy and hold one corner each. The mother elephant lays her trunk on her baby's back. I'm sure she knows they are trying to help.

When Ben nods they all start to lift, and slowly she is drawn up to stand. 'Let's hold her for a minute until she gets her legs steady,' says Ben.

We all stand and wait.

The calf steadies herself then slowly takes a tiny step, then another. Her little trunk swings and knots and twists and pokes. It's like she doesn't know how to control it, but it's so cute to watch.

She finds her mother's enormous face with it and wraps it around the middle of her mum's trunk. Slowly the men lower the cloth.

'She's standing by herself!' whispers Chelsea.

‘Now we just need her to drink some milk,’ says Peter.

And then, ever so slowly, the little calf shuffles to her mother’s side. Her trunk explores and her mouth finally finds what she needs: a long, warm drink of milk.

Ben turns and smiles at the group of teary-eyed onlookers. I turn around to look behind me and I see Mum. I slide past the others and give her a huge hug.

‘Well, I think you just saw something most vets will never see,’ says Mum quietly, hugging me right back.

A newspaper photographer is let in

to take a photo of the newborn baby, and Ben lets us stand in the photo.

'Is my hair okay?' fusses Chelsea.

'Perfect,' I say. 'You look like a world-famous animal trainer and groomer.'

'And you look just like a vet!' laughs Chelsea.

In the car on the way home Chelsea and I tell Mum about every single thing we've seen and done today. She is very impressed.

Chelsea is in the middle of telling Mum about the blue ribbon on Grandpa the tortoise when she falls asleep against my shoulder, and there, out of the corner of my eye I see . . . a cricket climbing out of her shirt!

Chelsea was right, there was one in there still!

1. **What did the sun bears eat at the zoo?**
a. Porridge
b. Honey
c. Sunshine
d. Bamboo

2. **What do you need to look in a giraffe's ear?**
a. Binoculars
b. A helicopter
c. A long neck
d. A ladder or platform

3. **Tamarins are a type of:**
a. Turtle
b. Monkey
c. Fruit
d. Meerkat

4. **Why is it dangerous to feed otters?**
a. They have terrible breath
b. They are too big
c. They have sharp teeth
d. They are too slippery

5. **Penguins won't eat fish that are:**
a. Bent
b. Orange
c. Smelly
d. Cute

6. The walnuts are hidden in plastic containers for:

a. Zebras

b. Snakes

c. Capuchin monkeys

d. Sun bears

7. Which of these animals has a shell?

a. Giraffe

b. Elephant

c. Zebra

d. Tortoise

8. Why do some baby animals have to be hand-raised?

a. Their mother dies

b. They get lost

c. Their mother has too many babies

d. Any of the above

9. Which of these baby animal orphans might you have to bottle feed?

a. A baby meerkat

b. A baby blue-tongue lizard

c. A tadpole

d. A baby goldfish

10. Baby elephants can usually stand up:

a. At one day old

b. Almost straight away

c. At three months of age

d. At one year of age

Answers : 1a, 2d, 3b, 4c, 5a, 6c, 7d, 8d, 9a, 10b. Well done!

My best friend Chelsea and I ♥ animals. I have a dog Curly and two guinea pigs, but we need more pets if I'm going to learn to be a vet. Today, we had the best idea ever . . . We're going to have a pet sleepover!

Chelsea and I are helping our friend, Maisy, get her pony ready for the local show. But Midgie is more interested in eating than in learning to jump (sigh). Pony training is a bit more difficult than we thought!

It's Spring and all the animals on Maisy's farm are having babies. Maisy says I can stay for a whole week and help out. There are chicks and ducklings hatching, orphan lambs to feed, and I can't wait for Bella to have her calf!

A terrible bushfire has struck and Mum's vet clinic is in chaos. Every day more injured animals arrive. Chelsea and I have never been busier! There's an adorable baby koala to feed by hand, a fat little wombat to bandage, and a funny blue-tongued lizard that Max is determined to make his pet.

It's the holidays and we're going camping by the beach. I'm bringing my vet-kit just in case. Vets needs to be prepared. I can't wait to toast marshmallows by the campfire, swim and explore – there are so many amazing animals at the beach.

I've won a competition to be a zookeeper for a day! My best friend Chelsea is coming too. I can't wait to learn all about the zoo animals. There will be meerkats, tigers and penguins to feed. And maybe some zoo vets who need some help (I must remember my vet-kit!).

There was a huge storm last night and now there are lots of lost dogs. One turned up outside my window (he must have known I'm nearly a vet). Luckily, Chelsea, Mum and I are helping out at the Lost Dogs' Home.

Juliet nearly a Vet Playground Pets

Chelsea and I have such a cool school – we get to have playground pets! Guinea pigs, lizards, fish and insects are all part of our science room. But this week we have a replacement teacher, and Miss Fine doesn't know much about animals. Luckily we do (it's so handy being nearly a vet)!

From Rebecca Johnson

My first holiday job was selling ice-creams at a small suburban zoo. The pay was lousy, but I didn't care because I got to wander around at lunchtime to look at all the animals. Juliet would have loved this job too. It makes me so happy to see how much zoos have changed and how well the animals are cared for. I still love going to zoos, and in Australia we are really lucky to have some of the best in the world.

From Kyla May

As a little girl, I always wanted to be a vet. I had mice, guinea pigs, dogs, goldfish, sea snails, sea monkeys and tadpoles as pets. I loved looking after my friends' pets when they went on holidays, and every Saturday I helped out at a pet store.

Now that I'm all grown up, I have the best job in the world. I get to draw lots of animals for children's books and for animated TV shows. In my studio I have two dogs, Jed and Evie, and two cats, Bosco and Kobe, who love to watch me draw.